TO AUDREY

FOR ALL THE FUN WE HAD

Copyright © 1995 by Jill Murphy

First U.S. edition 1995

Library of Congress Cataloging-in-Publication Data
Murphy, Jill
The last noo-noo / Jill Murphy.—1st U.S. ed.
Summary: His grandmother thinks he is too big to have a pacifier,
his mother agrees, and the other children make fun of him,
but Marlon will not give up until he is ready.
ISBN 1-56402-581-0
[1. Pacifiers (Infant care)—Fiction.   2. Mothers and sons—
Fiction.   3. Grandmothers—Fiction.]   I. Title.
PZ7.M9534Las   1995
[E]—dc20   94-48927

2 4 6 8 10 9 7 5 3 1

Printed in Italy

The pictures in this book were done in pen and pencil crayon.

Candlewick Press
2067 Massachusetts Avenue
Cambridge, Massachusetts 02140

THE LAST
NOO-NOO

Jill Murphy

CANDLEWICK PRESS
CAMBRIDGE, MASSACHUSETTS

M arlon sat on the floor watching TV. Marlon's granny sat in the armchair, watching Marlon. "He's getting too old for that pacifier," she said sternly to Marlon's mom.

"It's a noo-noo," said Marlon.

"He calls it a noo-noo," explained Marlon's mom.
"Well, what*ever* he calls it," said Marlon's granny,
"he looks ridiculous with that stupid big *thing*
    stuck in his mouth all the time."
"He doesn't have it *all* the time," soothed Marlon's
    mom. "Only at night or if he's a little tired.
        He's a little tired now—aren't you, sweetie?"
            "Mmmmm," said Marlon.

"His teeth will start sticking out," warned Marlon's granny.

"Monsters' teeth stick out anyway," observed Marlon.

"Don't answer back," said Marlon's granny. "You should just throw them *all* away," she continued. "At this rate he'll be starting school with a pacifier. At this rate he'll be starting work with a pacifier. You'll just have to be firm with him."

"Well," said Marlon's mom, "I am *thinking* about it. We'll start next week, won't we Marlon? Now that you're a big boy, we'll just get rid of all those noo-noos, won't we?"

"No," said Marlon.

"You see!" said Marlon's granny. "One word from you and he does as he likes."

There was no doubt about it. Marlon was a hopeless case.

Marlon's mom decided to take drastic action.
She gathered up every single noo-noo she could
find and dumped them all in the trash can
five minutes before the garbage truck arrived.
But Marlon had made plans just in case the worst
should happen. He had secret noo-noo supplies
all over the house.

There was a
yellow one down
the side of
the armchair,

a blue one at the back
of the bread box,

various different types
in his toy ambulance,

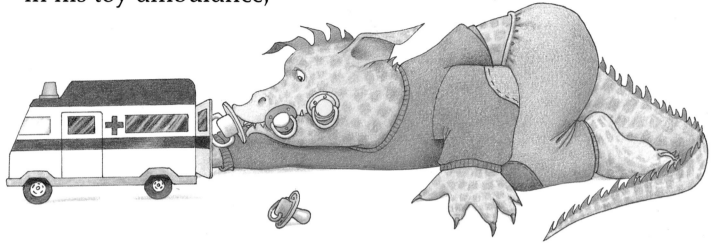

and his favorite
pink one was
lurking in the
toe of his boot.

His mother and granny were astonished.
They could not think where he kept finding them.
"You'll be teased when you go out to play,"
warned his granny. "A great big monster
like you with a baby's pacifier."
Marlon knew about this already. The other
monsters had been teasing him for ages, but he
loved his noo-noos so much that he didn't care.

The other monsters often lay in wait
and jumped out on Marlon as he
passed by with his noo-noo twirling.
"Who's a big baby, then?"
jeered Basher.
"Does the little baby

need his pacifier?" Alligatina sneered.
"Who's his mommy's little darling?"
cooed Boomps-a-Daisy.
Marlon always ignored their taunts.
"You're just jealous," he replied.
"You all wish you had one, too."

Gradually, the secret supply of noo-noos dwindled. Marlon's mom refused to buy any more, and they all began to be lost or thrown away by Marlon's mom. Finally, there was only one left—the pink one. Marlon kept it with him all the time—either in his mouth or under his pillow or in the toe of his boot, where no one thought to look.

To his delight, Marlon found one extra noo-noo that his mom had missed. It was a blue one that had fallen down the side of his bed and been covered up by a sock. He knew his best pink noo-noo wouldn't last forever, so he crept out and planted the blue one in the garden.

All the other monsters decided
to gang up on Marlon. They
collected lots of different pieces of
junk and fixed them all together
until they had made just
what they wanted. It was
a noo-noo snatcher.

Then they waited behind a bush
until Marlon came past with his
pink noo-noo twirling.
"Here he comes," said Alligatina.
"Grab it!" yelled Boomps-a-Daisy.
"Now!" said Basher.

With one quick hooking
movement, they caught
the ring of the noo-noo
with the noo-noo snatcher
and pulled!

But Marlon clenched his teeth and held on. Monsters have the most powerful jaws in the world. Once they have decided to hang on, that's *it*. Marlon hung on, the monsters hung on to the noo-noo snatcher, and there they stayed, both sides pulling with all their monster might.

And there they would *still* be, if Marlon had not decided, just at that very moment, that perhaps he *was* too old to have a noo-noo anymore.

So, he let go. And all the other monsters went whizzing off down the road, across the park, and into the pond with a mighty splash.

Marlon went home. "I've given up my noo-noo,"
he said. "I sort of threw it into the pond."

"Good gracious me!" exclaimed Marlon's mom,
sitting down suddenly with the shock.

"I told you," said Marlon's granny. "You just
have to be firm."

"Actually," said Marlon, "I've planted one, so I'll
have a noo-noo tree—just in case I change my mind."

"That's nice, dear," said Marlon's mom.

"Nonsense!" said Marlon's granny. "Pacifiers don't grow on trees. A noo-noo tree! How ridiculous!"